ishi

simple tips from a solid friend

photography and words by Akiko Yabuki

art direction by Yuko Brown

Brooklyn, NY

ishi: simple tips from a solid friend

Published by POW!
a division of powerHouse Packaging & Supply, Inc.
32 Adams Street, Brooklyn, NY 11201-1021

www.POWKidsBooks.com
Distributed by powerHouse Books
www.powerHouseBooks.com

Library of Congress Control Number: 2016930617

ISBN 978-1-57687-816-3

Art direction by Yuko Brown

Printing and Binding By Toppan Leefung

10 9 8 7

Printed and bound in China

How to use this book

1. Enjoy the book.
2. Choose happiness.
3. Share your happiness.
4. Pass Ishi to a friend.
5. Enjoy their happiness.

About this book

Stinky days.
We all have them.
After having one too many,
I found Ishi.
Ishi became my rock.
Ishi gave me tips.
Simple tips.
Tips that made me happy.
I hope they make you happy too!

My name is Ishi.

Ishi: Means rock in Japanese
Birthday: February 16
Place of birth: Kanagawa, Japan
Zodiac sign: Aquarius
Height: 1.77 inches / 4.5 cm
Weight: 3 ounces / 85 grams
Facebook page: facebook.com/IshiTheRock
Website: IshiTheRock.com

When something feels impossible,

I sleep and rest. And I try again the next day!

When I feel bottled up,

I move my body. Run, swim, climb a tree!

When I feel stinky,

I treat myself to something yummy!

When I feel the pressure,

I close my eyes, and slowly, deeply, and quietly, breathe.

When I feel lonely like a leftover,

I reach out to my friends.

When I feel like a failure,

I remind myself that every experience makes me grow.

When I feel like I just need a break,

I take a break.

When I feel like I'm the only one who's different,

I remind myself that everyone is different.

When I feel stuck,

I tell myself to always move forward, never backwards.

When nothing makes me feel better,

I go outside. Nature has magic!

When I feel hopeless,

I surround myself with dreamers!

When I feel sad thinking about what's missing,

I remind myself to focus on what I have and appreciate it.

When I feel lost,

I lean on my friends.

When I feel empty,

I give.

When I feel unhappy,

I smile. Happiness will follow!

Happiness is a choice.

Be happy.

Happiness is contagious.

Pass it on.

This book was printed with the help of the
following happiness ambassadors! THANK YOU!

George Nguyen, Ian Thubron, Kimiko Yabuki, Koichiro Yabuki, Yoshiko Suma, Abha, Lincoln & Opal, Christopher Reynolds, Mama and Papa Reynolds, Alrick Dorett, Nisse Kreysing, Karyn Drews, The Duong-Tran Family, Amy Lederer, Jacqueline Ma, Antoine Da Cruz, Adri, R Sakagawa, Donna, Ginger Gorton & Aias Chambers, Julie Gorton, Tasha, Layla Forh, Ara Mamourian, Momo Bell, Dash & Noa, Manabu Nagaoka, Margarita & Dave Fontes, Patrick, Juanita, Christian, Harry, Quake, Gordon & Ella Tom, William & Charlotte, Shawnta Buckner, Chisato Ishizaki, Dan Bealey, Amy Miranda, Traci Lawson, Masouma Karimian, Kathleen Kahlon, Hiroshi Takeda, Pam, Kim and Bryce Hanson, Linh Thai & Kevin Yee, Marilyn Lawson, Kurt & Abby, The Kahn Family, Hillary Miller-Slawson, Cheryl DF09, Tomoko, Goichi & Ema, JPA, Beth Ryan, Alex Nguyen & Thu Hoang, Lucia Mancuso, Liam & Miles Masson, Huy Nguyen, Adam & Lizz Norikane, Hawkins Pham, Ben and Kate Barker, Charlotte Frizziola, Kei & Nancy Sasaki, June Lee, Rachel Mc Hugh, Adam Reczek, Jill, Taka Tsurutani, Meg Gilsten Hale, Rick, J.J., Major & Tasha, Naho Kamikawa, Keita Sato, Lenny & Esther, Ranita Anderson, Nathan Jurevicius, Dori, Los Daddy Fresh, YASU, For Claire Small, Jessica Ng & Phoebe Choe, Jonathan, Noko, Dat Huy Ta, Peter Lim, Emily Osborne, Matteo Rossi, Helen M, David Baron, Ken Takahashi, Henry, Phuong, Janie & Gracie Nguyen, Jane Wu, Marine Bourgeois, Diane Alarcon, Katherine Ellis, Monica Multari, Sandy Yarbrough, Gerry Cardinal III, CJ Sullivan, Ryotaro & Lisa Yabuki, Karin & Yujin, NINO, Susumu & Kaeko Tanimura, Mary Beth, Amber Ellis, Lee Saunders, Ding Sze Yi.